Mario AND THE COW

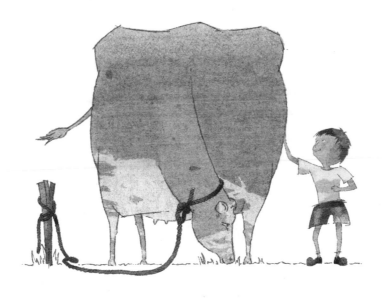

D1160095

for Rafi

Library of Congress Cataloging-in-Publication Data
Names: Ortiz, Miguel Antonio, author.
Title: Mario and the cow / by Miguel Antonio Ortiz.
Description: Maplewood, New Jersey : Irene Weinberger Books, an imprint of
Hamilton Stone Editions, [2019] | Summary: "In order to keep young Mario
busy for a while, his grandfather assigns him the task of looking after a
cow that's tethered to a stake in the pasture"-- Provided by publisher.
Identifiers: LCCN 2018040577 | ISBN 9780979598661 (pbk. : alk. paper)
Subjects: | CYAC: Grandfathers--Fiction. | Cows--Fiction. | Chores--Fiction.
Classification: LCC PZ7.1.O785 Mar 2019 | DDC [E]--dc23
LC record available at https://lccn.loc.gov/2018040577

Irene Weinberger Books

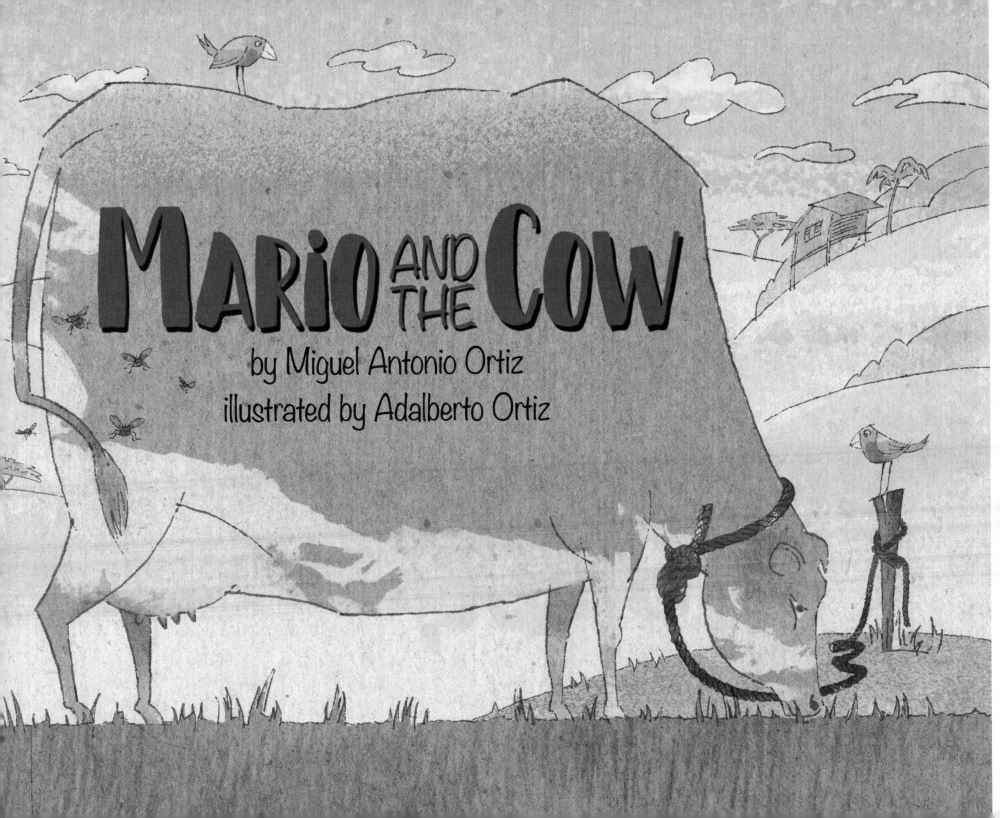

Mario and the Cow

by Miguel Antonio Ortiz

illustrated by Adalberto Ortiz

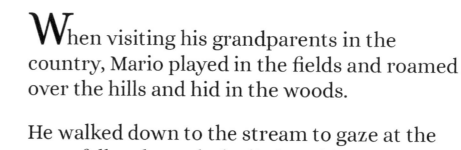

When visiting his grandparents in the country, Mario played in the fields and roamed over the hills and hid in the woods.

He walked down to the stream to gaze at the waterfall and watch the little golden fish dart about in the sandy pools.

Sometimes he climbed up trees to look at baby birds in their nests.

Mario was on holiday, but everyone else had chores to do. He tagged along with one person or another and helped with whatever they were doing.

Grandpa was going to hoe the field on the other side of the hill. Mario followed him.

"I have just the right job for you," Grandpa said as they walked into a clearing where a cow was tied with a very long rope to a stake in the ground.

"I need someone to watch this cow and see that she doesn't get into any mischief. Do you think you can do that?"

"Sure," Mario said, "I can do that."

"Remember, she has to stay tied to that stake."

"I'll remember," Mario said.

Mario sat on a stump to watch the cow.
Grandpa, hoe in hand, walked off to work in
the sweet potato patch.

Mario sat on the stump for a very long time.
The cow grazed leisurely, first in one spot
then in another.

She paid no attention to Mario.

Mario got tired of sitting. He chased a butterfly through the field until it flew too high. He lay down on the ground to watch the clouds change shapes. Up there he saw a lion and a dragon and then a very large steamship like the one he had seen when he had been to San Juan Harbor with his father.

He got tired of watching the sky, the clouds, and the field.

The cow ate all the grass around the stake as far as the rope would let her. Mario thought of how hungry she would be with nothing more to eat. If only she could reach another patch of fresh grass.

Of course Grandpa had said not to untie the rope, but maybe he meant not to untie the cow's end of the rope.

If he untied the rope from the stake, he could lead the cow around the field to a better grazing spot.

He had no trouble untying the rope. He led
the cow to where there was more grass.

Yes, this was a very good thing he was doing
for the cow. He felt very important holding
onto the rope with the cow at the other end.

The cow decided to take a longer stroll.
Mario felt the tug. "Oh well, we can take a
walk as long as I hold onto the rope," he said
to himself.

The cow walked faster. Mario tugged on the rope. The cow did not stop. Mario pulled even harder, but the cow kept walking. He dug his heels into the ground and leaned back so that the cow would feel all his weight.

She kept on walking.

He was sorry that he had untied her, but there was nothing to do now but hold on.

He lost his balance, but he still held on. The cow continued her walk. Mario held on tighter, but now...

... his stomach was on the ground and the cow kept walking. The rough ground scraped his chest and stomach. He was afraid that if he let go of the rope, ... the cow would wander away and get lost.

Finally the cow stopped. Mario looked around. The stake was on the other side of the field. He had to get the cow back to that spot and retie the rope.

He sat on the ground for a while. Then he stood up and pulled on the rope. To his surprise, the cow was ready to follow him. He led her all the way back...

. . . and tied the rope securely to the stake.

Happy, he did a little dance and patted the cow. He would have hugged her, but she was too big to get his arms around her.

The sun hung low over the hills on the western edge of the field. Hoe over his shoulder, Grandpa returned from the sweet potato patch. He glanced at the cow and at the knot Mario had tied.

"Good job," he said to Mario.

"Thank you," Mario replied.

"You got a little dirty," Grandpa said as they walked back to the house.

Mario looked down at his shirt and pants. "Just a little," he said.

"Can't be helped," Grandpa said. "A man goes out to watch a cow, he gets pretty dirty. That's the way it is."

"You're right," Mario said. "It's just a little bit of dirt. No big deal."

"That's right," Grandpa said.

From that day on, Mario thought twice about doing anything he had been told not to do.

CPSIA information can be obtained at www.ICGtesting.com
Printed in the USA
BVIW120752251118
533572BV00061B/547

9780979598661